BEEP! BEEP! Go to Sleep!

by **Todd Tarpley**   illustrated by **John Rocco**

L **B**
Little, Brown and Company
New York Boston

Three little robots, time for bed.

Time to dim your infrared.

Brush your rotors 'round and 'round.

Clean your shields . . .

. . . and power down.

Quiet at last, not a peep.

Three little robots are . . .

Three little robots back to bed.

Quiet at last, not a peep.

Three little robots are . . .

Quiet at last, not a peep.

Three little robots are . . .

Quiet at last, not a peep.

Three little robots are . . .

Somewhere there are
robots beeping,
buzzing-bouncing,
squawking-squeaking.

Blipping-bopping,
blinking-boinking,
winking-whirring,
even oinking.

But not these robots
snuggled deep. . . .